Geraldine Durrant

Pirate Gran
Goes for Gold

illustrated by Rose Forshall

Gran's **great** at sport.

"When I was a pirate I could run 100 metres quicker than you can say doubloon," says Gran, "especially with a policeman after me."

So Gran's invited her old shipmates Flint-Hearted Jack, Fingers O'Malley and Cut-throat Malone to help her train for the Olympics.

I heard her shout "Avast there me hearties" when they were running round the garden baton-passing this afternoon but **someone** kept dropping it.

Gran's very loyal so she won't say
who, but I notice she's been calling
the bosun **Butterfingers** O'Malley.

She's knitted special striped costumes for the synchronised swimming, and she and her pet crocodile have already made quite a splash at the pool.

Mind you, when she saw the headline *Man-eater Terrifies Toddlers* in the paper Gran was **furious**.

"My pet crocodile is good with children, and has never eaten anyone who didn't deserve it," said Gran.

I think her jumping looks
very promising.

She's been using the clothes prop to
pole-vault over the washing line . . .

...and land in the compost heap.

"It's one small step for a Gran," she said dusting off the cabbage leaves, "one giant leap for Grankind."

Of course pole-vaulting isn't for everyone, but Gran says if you don't mind feeling dizzy and showing your knickers it's a sport more Grans should think about.

Grandpa banned bowling after
one of Gran's cannon balls blew
up his greenhouse.

With him in it.

"Lot of fuss about nothing," Gran grumbled after
she'd rescued him. "The day I can't haul an old man
out of an apple tree is the day I hang up my flintlock."

But even Grandpa admits she is **brilliant** at showjumping – although it is the first time he's seen it done on a crocodile.

There's no doubt Gran's a crack shot with her blunderbuss.

"Show me a varmint at 50 paces, and I'll show you a man with a hole through his hat," laughed Gran after she'd fired at Grandpa's scarecrow.

She's **really** good at fencing too.

Grandpa challenged her to a duel
with a cucumber...

and Gran sliced it into
sandwiches with her cutlass.

And she's claiming the world record for the fastest Gran over 800 metres –

although Grandpa still says it doesn't count if you have been fired out of a cannon.

I'd love to see Gran standing under a
Jolly Roger listening to a sea shanty
when she gets a gold medal.

But Gran says the most important thing isn't winning, it's taking part and having fun.

So just in case Grandpa is going to make her
a special medal from all of us – for being the
world's Champion Gran.

For my crew: Patrick & Jimmy, Barnaby & Julia, Toby & Jo, Jez & Becca, Eleanor & Alice.

The first book of Pirate Gran was developed from the winning entry to the
BBC London / RaW 60-second story-writing competition. RaW is the BBC's
biggest ever campaign to help adults across the UK to build their confidence
in reading and writing, by telling stories to their children.

A CIP catalogue record for this book is available from Library and Archives Canada.

First published in the UK in 2010 by the National Maritime Museum, Greenwich, London SE10 9NF

www.nmm.ac.uk/publishing

Text © 2010 Geraldine Durrant and illlustrations © 2010 Rose Forshall

Design Kayt Manson and project management Sara Ayad

www.breakwaterbooks.com

Paperback 978-1-55081-446-0

Printed in China